A Fitting End

A Mallard Melodrama
Book 1

R J Williams

For my wife, Jenni, with love

Other books by R J Williams

Death in Earnest

Sovereign Risk

Chapter 1

Verity Mallard heard a door slam and put down her book. She looked out on Montagu Square, wet and gloomy in the November dusk.

A hansom cab drew away as its passenger strode casually across the pavement and up the steps to the front door. She waited while her visitor took off his hat and coat.

"Is the business concluded, brother?"

"Most satisfactorily, if I may say so. No unpleasant mess or loose ends."

"Excellent. Now Mortie, do take yourself off. I have an article to write. The gory details will have to wait."

"Wait? Dear God, Verity, you act as though this was an everyday happening. Is it not the most portentous event in both our lives?"

"Yes, my dear, and if we are to ensure that it does not come back to haunt us, we must behave as though it had never occurred. You may tell me all later."

Mortimer raised his eyebrows but knew that there was little point in arguing. "Very well, I'll go and read the newspapers in the back parlour, shall I?"

Receiving no response, he left the room.

Verity sat at her writing desk and took up her pen. The article she'd promised the editor of *The Englishwoman's Review* was overdue. A reflection on Mary Wollstonecraft's

Vindication of the Rights of Woman from the perspective of the modern struggle for women's suffrage. She must set herself to complete the task.

A bare paragraph was all she managed. Returning to the window, she stared into the darkness. As Mortimer had said, the business was over, and what a business it was.

The murders had ceased abruptly, a few weeks after they'd begun. 'The Autumn of Terror' they called it. That was seven years ago. Five women cruelly butchered. Women of ill-repute as the popular press had it. Easy prey. There had been further killings of women in Whitechapel, which raised the spectre that the Ripper might have resumed his grim occupation. But, in the end, it was decided that these were just ordinary murders, nothing to excite the frenzy of fear and suspicion that Jack had caused between August and November 1888.

Five poor wretches, living from hand to mouth in hovels and grimy common lodging houses, or submitting to the cold charity of the workhouse. Their lives were a daily struggle for survival. They'd do whatever was necessary to scrape together a few coins to pay for food, lodgings, and the drink that numbed the bleak reality of their lives.

Verity was horrified and repelled by the lurid descriptions of mutilated bodies in the newspapers. Her comfortable existence was far removed from the squalor of the East End, but she couldn't escape the unease that affected women of all classes. The thought that a pitiless, calculating killer was at large.

Her day-to-day life at that time: her first steps in journalism, her visits to museums and galleries, and her good works at Bart's hospital were undertaken within the safe and respectable streets of genteel London. However, the beggars and street sellers she passed were a constant reminder of that other London, whose inhabitants scratched a precarious living from their well-to-do neighbours.

She felt compelled to take an interest in one or two of these unfortunates, stopping to pass the time of day and pressing a few coppers on them. One, in particular, a short, plump, middle-aged woman, caught her attention. Perhaps it was the small spark of hope she thought she saw behind the pallid face, or the way she responded to a few kind words. Some drew away and others barked obscenities at her, but this one sat and listened with a hint of a smile and, little by little, revealed something of her story.

She'd been married, she said, bore three children, but young John was born a cripple and put in an institution and Emily died at the age of twelve. Annie had never been the same since; 'drink took hold of me' as she put it, drawing her away from her marriage and her remaining child. So, she found herself alone, supported by a few shillings from her estranged husband, but then he died and she sunk further into penury.

Now, she scratched out a bare existence selling crochet work and flowers on the street. Her name was Annie - Annie Chapman.

It was in late August 1888 that Verity had last spoken to her. She'd seemed unusually happy that day, 'enjoying the sun', she said. Verity felt glad for her and gave her a sixpence before rushing off to an appointment. The next time she saw that face was in a sensational depiction of the murder of the Ripper's second victim, plastered across the pages of the *Illustrated Police News*.

It had shaken her badly. Mortimer had been her great support, comforting her and taking her out of herself with his particular brand of irreverent humour, in which even the darkest of subjects had a comical side.

The efforts of the police to find the murderer came to nothing. They identified some suspects, but no evidence was forthcoming to support a prosecution. Rumours abounded and continued long after the murders ceased.

But now justice had finally been done. Not that the police or the public would ever know of it. The legend would live on, but only three people knew the truth, and that would never be discovered.

Chapter 2

Verity took her seat near the fireplace. Mortimer sat opposite, legs outstretched, gazing vacantly at the glass of amontillado in his hand. He was the younger of the pair by nine minutes, a fact that he was given to refer to from time to time to explain the difference in their natures. She - impulsive and energetic, he - languid and unruffled. "I was in no hurry to make an entrance, you see and, of course, manners dictate that it's ladies first," he'd say.

Life had drawn him along, rather. Winchester, then Oxford, a rowing half-blue and an unspectacular law degree and here he was - a junior barrister in law chambers in the City. For recreation, he had the Unicorn Club and an occasional appearance with the bat at Twickenham Cricket Club. While Verity had settled herself in their family townhouse, he'd established himself in comfortable lodgings in Chelsea.

"Now then, Mortimer, tell me; the business - it went as planned?"

"Yes, as planned."

"Benson played his part?"

"Perfectly."

"The body?"

"Went into the river just after midnight on an ebb tide. By daybreak, it would have been well downstream."

"We must keep an eye out for any reports of it being found."

"Yes, and if it's never found, so much the better."

"We'll have a proper celebration at the weekend. The Café Royal, I think."

"Capital. A toast?"

"Yes. Of course. Here's to the memory of Annie Chapman, God rest her soul."

"To Annie Chapman."

***

The business, as Verity referred to it, came about quite by chance. The Whitechapel Murders had taken place seven years earlier. But Jack the Ripper's murderous spree still exerted a powerful influence on the public imagination. Any murder of a woman of the lower classes in the city's east was likely to provoke fevered speculation in the press about whether Jack had resumed his ghastly activities.

Suspects had come and gone. Three, in particular: Montague Druitt, Aaron Kosminski, and Michael Ostrog, fell under suspicion, but nothing came of it.

As a junior member of chambers, it fell to Mortimer to undertake much of the work that more senior lawyers considered too mundane or insufficiently lucrative to bother with. Petty criminal cases were his chief responsibility, along with divorce proceedings. And it was one such case that brought Henry Reginald Powell into his orbit.

At the beginning of November, arriving back in his rooms after a leisurely lunch and a stroll along the embankment, Mortimer was accosted by Jimmy Allen, the head clerk.

"Nice little divorce case for you, sir. Mister Frimley thought it would be right up your alley he did."

"Thank you, Jimmy, too kind, I'm sure. Won't produce much of a fee, then?"

"Now, now, sir. You know I always do my best for you." Jimmy responded with a wink.

"Yes, of course, Jimmy, for which I am eternally grateful," Mortimer replied wearily. "Do wheel the client in, then."

Moments later, Jimmy ushered in a woman whose most memorable features were her unusual height, around six feet, and her face, whose elongated nose and chin, reminded Mortimer of the winner of the previous month's last race at Newmarket.

She was dressed stylishly in a princess gown of grey satin and her fair hair was topped by a simple black velvet bonnet. Forty years of age, Mortimer surmised, although her figure retained the hourglass shape of someone half her age.

"Mrs Clara Powell to see you, Mister Mallard," Jimmy said by way of introduction before leaving the room.

Mortimer rose, skirting his desk and extending his hand.

"Mrs Powell, I'm Mortimer Mallard. How may I be of assistance? Please take a seat."

Her gloved hand gripped his with unexpected pressure. She seated herself and spoke in a voice as forceful as her grip.

"You may assist me, Mister Mallard, by securing a divorce from my faithless, useless, and downright dissolute husband. That is what you can do for me, and the sooner the better."

Mortimer felt as though he was being pressed into his seat under the force of her opening broadside.

"I see, Mrs Powell."

"Do you? How can you possibly see? I have yet to provide you with any information on the nature of his … failings."

"Merely a turn of phrase, madam. Of course, I shall require you to elaborate in order to understand the essential facts of the matter," Mortimer responded hastily, wondering what on earth he was letting himself in for and vowing to have sharp words with Jimmy in due course.

Reaching for his fountain pen, he looked up and smiled, receiving a blank stare in response. "Let's begin with your husband's name."

"It's Henry. Henry Reginald Powell."

"And how long have you been married, may I ask?"

"Four years. Look here, I don't have time for all this back and forth. I will acquaint you with all the pertinent details and if you require anything further, you can ask. Is that clear?"

"Perfectly, madam, please go ahead," Mortimer said, promising himself a stiff brandy when the ordeal was over.

They'd met, she said, in South Africa. It was her second marriage, his first - as far as she was aware, she added pointedly. Her first husband had been a middle-ranking civil servant in the colonial administration at Cape Town, but he'd died suddenly in 1890. Henry had come out to the Cape in the previous year from England and found work as a reporter on *The Cape Argus*. He and her husband had become acquainted at a gentleman's club, and Henry had become a regular visitor at her home.

After her husband's death, she found work as a companion to a wealthy old spinster, which supplemented her small widow's pension and enabled her to rent out her house while she resided with her employer.

Although Henry had disappeared from her life after her husband's funeral, he'd suddenly called upon her some months afterwards and she, needing a friendly face and someone other than the old lady to talk to, had allowed herself to form an attachment with him.

"I'd not been considering marriage again, you know," she confided. But as the weeks passed, a mutual bond of affection grew between them. "He could be most solicitous and although I lack a sense of humour myself, I found him amusing, with a wealth of anecdotes and fascinating recollections. Pure inventions, as it turned out. Oh, and if I'm honest with myself, I felt sympathy for his disability."

"Disability? What was the nature of this disability?"

"His hand. His left hand had been amputated. A carriage accident, he said."

"I see. Please go on."

Then her world was upended by the sudden death of her employer in a fall at her home. "I found her at the foot of the stairs one morning. I can still see the look of surprise on her face, lying there in an undignified heap and quite cold to the touch."

Her belligerent manner had gradually softened as she spoke and, at this point, she put a hand to her throat, struggling to breathe.

"My dear Mrs Powell, are you feeling unwell? Here, let me fetch you a glass of water." Mortimer turned to a side table on which rested a carafe and two glasses. Filling one, he handed it to her.

She took a sip of water and composed herself.

Henry proposed within days of the old lady's death, and Clara accepted. "I was in a low state at the time, so I said yes. I'm not so sure that I would have done so if I was in my normal state of mind. The legacy was such a surprise. I was shocked. I had no expectations."

"Legacy," Mortimer exclaimed. "My word, this gets more interesting by the minute."

Having no living relatives, the old lady bequeathed half her estate to Clara and the remainder to several charities.

"I've got to hand it to him. He said that he'd quite understand if I changed my mind about marriage. An empty gesture, of course. He calculated that I'd go ahead with it. Mind you, I did have second thoughts, but the wedding went ahead."

"Hmm – but you did not remain in South Africa."

"Only for six months. I'd a hankering to return to England. Neither of us had family in South Africa, and he said he had none in England either. In fact, he tried to talk me out of coming back, but I wouldn't be dissuaded."

"And what happened after you returned?"

"We bought, or rather, I bought, a small house in Highgate. The legacy was sufficient to maintain us in a modestly comfortable style, but we agreed that he should find employment."

"As a newspaper reporter?"

"Yes, he'd been a successful reporter on *The Star*, he said, and I expected that he would seek employment there again."

"Did that not occur?"

"Well, he gave me the impression that he'd obtained a position there, but the truth is that he was only employed on a casual basis, and not by *The Star*, but by one or two less salubrious journals. I could never get to the bottom of it, but I'm convinced that *The Star* would not have him back. This was the first sign that perhaps he was not all he pretended to be.

"To begin with, he'd leave each day as though going to work and return in the evenings. I suppose that went on for about two years. Indeed, we lived a largely normal life. Made friends, went visiting, and had evenings out at the theatre. I introduced him to my family. I have a brother and two sisters, but none of them would take to him and, in the end, I found it easier to visit them alone. Then he took to staying out for hours, well into the night sometimes, telling me that he was working on some story or other. Eventually, he would be away for days and when I questioned him about it, he'd say he'd been sent on a special assignment by his editor. At first, it worried me but after a time I became resigned to it.

"Whenever I tried to take an interest in his work, he'd be evasive, rarely mentioning any stories that he was reporting on and fobbing me off."

"So, you grew apart."

"Yes. I came to my senses and told him I wouldn't countenance him leading a double life, which is what it seemed to me."

"How did he take it?"

"I think he was expecting it. He said he found living with me was holding him back. He could not pursue his career to its full advantage without being free to come and go as he pleased without my interference. Interference, if you please - the gall of the man."

"Did this cause a separation?"

"Yes, I packed his bags for him and put them on the doorstep."

"So, you have been separated for how long?"

"Twenty months. I saw nothing of him for six months and then he appeared at my door, begging me to have him back. He cut a sorry figure, I must say, although now I'm sure that was largely contrived. He swore he'd changed. That he realised he'd wronged me. All the usual excuses. No doubt you've heard them all before, Mr Mallard."

"Yes, they have an all too familiar ring to them. What was the outcome?"

"Well, I didn't have him back, no fear of that, but I was persuaded to make him a small allowance, if only to be rid of him. That had some effect; he'd taken lodgings in Paddington. I sent him a monthly postal order."

"Let me guess, Mrs Powell, he wanted more?"

"After a few months, yes, back he came again. Turned up at my door, the worse for drink. He started on the same routine as before, trying to win my sympathy, but when I refused, he became angry, seriously angry. The language wasn't even fit for the barrack room. I'm not easily intimidated, Mr Mallard, but it frightened me. I threatened to call a constable, but that only enraged him all the more. If my neighbour Mr Johnson and his son had not appeared, I think he might have attacked me."

"The man's clearly a blackguard. Did you go to the police?"

"Yes, I went straight round the next morning. The sergeant was quite sympathetic but said that unless Henry had laid a hand on me, there was little he could do. 'We can't involve ourselves in every domestic argument or we'd do little else,' he said."

"Hmm – I'm afraid that is generally the attitude of our police."

"I should have cut off his allowance there and then, but to tell the truth, I was fearful that it would precipitate another outburst. A few months went by and I prayed that he'd decided to leave me alone. Then I found out that he'd been running up debts and giving my name as some sort of guarantor. I have had debt collectors calling. It's got to stop. I should have pressed for divorce as soon as I knew of his true character, I know. Now, I must beg you to help me to be rid of him for good."

"Mrs Powell, I will be pleased to act for you, but a divorce is not easy to obtain and we must assume that your husband will not be amenable. Have you any reason to suppose that he has committed adultery?"

"I have every reason to think so. He taunted me, saying that he had many female admirers. I have no proof, however."

"Well, I imagine, given the nature of the man, that adultery will certainly be occurring and if so, we must find proof. Indeed, we must find out all we can about his conduct, because the best chance of success is to be able to paint a picture of a thoroughly vile man."

"I see, and if adultery could be proved, then I could be free of the wretch?"

"Ah, would that it were that straightforward, Mrs Powell. As it stands, the Matrimonial Causes Act, the law that deals with divorce, places a greater burden on women who file for divorce than it does on men. Regrettably, while it allows a man to seek a divorce solely on the grounds of a wife's infidelity, the same cannot be said for a wife."

"What on earth do you mean? Does the law not apply equally? Surely, adultery is adultery."

"The man or woman in the street would no doubt see it in those terms, madam, but our legislators, in their wisdom, have seen fit to place a greater burden on the wife. It means that in addition to adultery, you would need another cause."

"Such as?"

"Well, please excuse the indelicacy of the terms, but they include incest and rape."

Clara Powell's back stiffened. "Wretch that he is, I have no reason to suspect such depravity."

"Then there's desertion, cruelty, or bigamy," Mortimer added. "From what you've told me, it may be construed that your husband has deserted you, but of course, he may very well contest that, citing his attempt to return to you, for example. Also, your continued financial support could be seen by a court as being an indication that you were content to maintain a relationship with the man, albeit a purely financial one. However, let's proceed on the basis that desertion is arguable.

"Cruelty may also be difficult. The episode in which he harangued you on your doorstep may be cited, and the fact that there were witnesses is in your favour, but to make a case of cruelty based on that one occurrence is not a realistic proposition.

"Then there is bigamy, of course. What's not to say that he may have another wife somewhere? There are ways of discovering if that is the case. But the first step must be to discover proof of adultery."

"I've told you all I know, Mr Mallard. I fail to see how I can furnish the proof to which you refer."

"No indeed, madam, of course, you can't. But, if you would leave things in my hands, I will set in train certain inquiries. The man's life will be laid bare."

"You mean a private investigator, I assume?"

"Yes, I have such an associate. A person of the highest integrity and absolute discretion, I can assure you."

"That will incur more expense."

"Yes, there's no denying that. However, if we are to take the matter further, there's no alternative, I'm afraid. Please take your time to think it over."

"Oh, thinking it over will make no difference. I can't bear to allow things to continue as they are. You have my agreement to proceed. Please furnish me with a statement of your fees. I will require a report on the progress of these inquiries no later than ten days from now. Does that seem appropriate?"

"Eminently so, Mrs Powell. If you would be so good as to provide me with your husband's last known address, Paddington, wasn't it? And do you also have a photograph of the fellow?"

With the address having been supplied, together with a promise to send round a photograph, Mrs Powell was shown out of Mortimer's office.

Five minutes later, he emerged. Passing Jimmy Allen in the corridor, he called out. "I'm off to see Benson."

Chapter 3

Mortimer's law chambers had used George Benson's services for several years whenever discreet inquiries were to be made. A veteran of the Anglo-Egyptian War, he'd served for fifteen years in the King's Royal Rifle Corps. Twice wounded in action, he'd retired from the army in the rank of sergeant.

For three years he drifted around the United States, including a spell working for the Pinkerton Detective Agency, where his activities often walked a fine line between genuine law enforcement and criminality.

He'd come to the conclusion, rightly or wrongly, that there were times when justice could not be achieved by keeping within the strict confines of the law. On his return to England, he put his knowledge and experience to work on his own account.

This case had started like most others. Mortimer called around and briefed him. The information obtained from Clara Powell was passed to him: the man's name, his photograph, and an address in Paddington. Beyond that, he knew only that Henry Powell had done some work for a couple of journals of the racier kind.

His starting point was the Paddington address, but there he drew a blank. After observing the house for a whole day without seeing any sign of Powell, he'd knocked on the door. The stout middle-aged man who answered looked at him with suspicion. "Yes, what's your business here?" he said sharply.

"I hope you may be able to tell me whether a cousin of mine lives here. I carelessly lost the address he gave me. I do recall that he said he was lodging in this street, but I can't, for the life of me, recall the number."

"Cousin, eh? Hope his name's not Henry Powell. Damned scoundrel disappeared owing me rent and making off with my late father's gold watch and some silver items as well. Never trusted the man. Shifty character, he was. I only let him lodge here because my wife took pity on him having only one hand."

"My cousin's name is Tom Prentice."

"Oh, no, there's no one of that name here, and I'm sorry to sound off at you like that, but I'm furious about the way he betrayed us, and the police were no use either."

George raised his hat and left.

With no other lead to follow, he called the next day at the offices of the two scandal sheets mentioned in Mortimer's briefing. At *The Weekly Exposé*, his question as to the whereabouts of Henry Powell produced a brusque response from the Editor.

"Don't mention that damned wastrel to me. Haven't set eyes on the man in the last month and good riddance, I say."

At *The People's Enquirer*, he got into conversation with a young man rushing out of the office as he made his entrance. A mild collision ensued. George offered profuse apologies as he picked up the young fellow's hat and enquired whether he was in that journal's employ. The young man's initial reluctance to provide any information was overcome by the offer of a half-crown for his trouble. Within minutes, George was in possession of the following facts. Yes, the young man was a junior reporter. Yes, Henry Powell had worked there. No, he hadn't seen Henry lately. No, he didn't know his address, but Henry had been known to frequent several of the public houses in and around Fleet Street, *The Old Bell* being a particular favourite.

Later that day, George left his vantage point behind a dray cart and walked a dozen paces behind the figure that emerged from *The Old Bell*. Dressed like any city clerk, he blended into the streetscape.

At 5.30 pm, the pavement was filled with workers making their way home. George kept his eyes on the man ahead of him.

Turning onto New Bridge Street, his quarry quickened his pace, heading south toward Blackfriars Bridge. Forty years old, with dark hair and beard, a sallow complexion, five foot ten, solid build, along with one other singular characteristic, a pinned-up left sleeve. A perfect match to the sepia photograph George carried, in which Henry Reginald Powell stood stiffly at the side of his seated wife.

Over Blackfriars Bridge they went, then along Blackfriars Road until Henry struck off to the west. A few minutes later, he stopped at the front door of a house in a terrace of identical dark brick dwellings on Whittlesey Street. George watched from across the road as Henry opened the door and went inside.

In a moment, he crossed and strolled along the terrace.

The houses faced directly onto the street. Each had two windows on the ground floor, one on each side of the front door, and an upper storey with three windows, evenly spaced.

Passing the house in question, a neatly printed card in one of the ground-floor windows caught his eye.
Mrs Elizabeth Follett's Guest House
For Respectable Gentlemen.
Apply Within

A slight grey-haired woman wearing a dark dress and bonnet answered his knock.

"Yes sir, can I help you?" She looked him up and down through black-rimmed spectacles.

George again used the fictitious cousin enquiry.

"Oh, cousin, you say? I've only two guests at present. Old Mr Stanislavski's been with me for years and there's a new gentleman. What is the name of your cousin?"

"Prentice, Tom Prentice is his name."

"No, my new lodger's called Powell. Sorry, I can't help you. You could try number thirty-six. They take in lodgers. Perhaps he's there."

As she spoke, a man appeared from the rear of the house. George could see him clearly and wondered whether he was making for the front door, but partway along the passage he turned and trudged up the stairs. It was Henry Powell, without a doubt. Not just a casual caller, but a resident at that address.

For appearance's sake, George walked along to number thirty-six and repeated the performance, then retraced his steps, crossing the Thames and heading north to Holborn and the small office from which he conducted his private investigation business.

There, he set to work preparing a report on his inquiries which he would send by courier to Mortimer Mallard the following morning. When he'd finished, he picked up his hat and left.

***

Stepping through the door of *The Lamb and Flag* in Covent Garden, George shoved his way through the press of drinkers to the back room and peered through a dense fug of tobacco smoke. Fearing that he'd be in for a long search of the area's many pubs and taverns, he was relieved to catch sight of the thin, weasel-faced form of Alfie Cotton.

Mr Alfred Cotton, at thirty years of age, was a man of many parts. Street seller, confidence trickster, handler of stolen goods, and font of all knowledge regarding the seamier side of London life. George had found in Alfie an excellent source of information, at a price, of course, but also a peerless resource when it came to keeping tabs on a target. Together with Alfie's younger brother, Dick, George had two unofficial assistants to call on when his workload proved too much for one person to handle. Now that he had Henry Powell's address, he'd need to keep the house under observation for a few days at least and to have the fellow followed whenever he left the place. That would take the three of them.

Chapter 4

Two days had passed, in which George and Alfie took turns keeping watch on Henry.

They sat together in a corner of *The Lamb and Flag*, mugs of porter at their elbows, scrutinising the notes that George had compiled.

Wednesday:

Observer – George

8.30 am - Leaves lodgings carrying a satchel. Calls at a pawnbroker on Blackfriars Road. Takes omnibus to Fleet Street. Spends morning visiting newspaper offices.

12.30 pm – Old Bell Tavern. Bread and cheese, then drinking in the public bar. Gets into conversation with a couple of other men but leaves alone at 4.35 pm.

4.50 pm – Arrives at the Embankment near Blackfriars Bridge. Walks slowly in the direction of Waterloo Bridge, accosting passers-by for money. Overheard claiming to have lost his hand at Majuba Hill. Has pinned a medal on his jacket.

6.05 pm – Crosses Waterloo Bridge. Calls at a pie shop near Waterloo Station.

6.20 pm - Enters the Cornwall Arms, Cornwall Street. Drinks alone. Leaves at 8.00 pm. Walks around the perimeter of Waterloo Station. Stops at a lock-up.

Produces a key and enters. Leaves at 9.20 pm and returns to lodgings.

Observation halted for the day.

"Hmm," said Alfie. "No sign of a fancy woman. Seems he's sniffing around Fleet Street trying to find work."

"Looks that way," agreed George, "but what else have we learned about him?"

"Not above begging, is he? Pretending to be a wounded ex-soldier, pretty low act," Alfie snorted. "And there's that visit to the pawnbrokers. Pound to a penny, he had the stolen items from his previous lodgings in that satchel."

"No doubt," George concurred, "but it's that last bit that's most interesting. I tried listening at the door of that Waterloo lock-up but didn't want to give the game away by staying there too long. There was a light on inside. I saw its glow under the door but no sound, so I've no idea what he was doing there."

"Keeps stolen goods there's my guess."

"Yes, perhaps that's it, Alfie, but he'd have to be doing a lot of thieving to need a lock-up of that size. Now then, let's see what we can make of his movements yesterday," George said, turning back to the notes in front of them.

Thursday:

Observer – Alfie

9.05 am – Leaves lodgings. Appears in no hurry. Walks at a leisurely pace east, stopping to look in shop windows. Calls at a tobacconist on Southwark Bridge Road. Proceeds to Borough Underground Station. Takes the train to the terminus at King William Street. Catches omnibus north along Bishopsgate, alighting near Spitalfields Market. Shelters from a shower of rain in

Bishopsgate Library. Reads the newspapers. Emerges at 11.45 am.

Walks through Spitalfields Market and crosses Commercial Street, then into Hanbury Street. Walks along slowly, looking at the house numbers. Stops and stands observing a house on the opposite side of the street. No 29.

Moves on after a few minutes.

12.05 pm – Stops a short distance away at the Ten Bells. Drinks alone. Takes out a notebook and spends some time making notes.

1.16 pm – leaves the Ten Bells and crosses Commercial Street turning into Dorset Street. Walks to the end of the street then doubles back, stopping at an alley called Miller's Court. Stands outside the door to No 13 as though listening for sounds within. Moves to a window. Looks around furtively and then peers inside but only for a few seconds.

1.25 pm – recrosses Commercial Street and heads east through side streets and alleyways. In Buck's Row, stops outside a house and turns to survey the opposite side of the street. The object of his attention appears to be a gateway between a row of cottages and a warehouse. Crosses the road to stand at the gateway, then abruptly turns away.

Walks to Whitechapel High Street, then heads west before crossing the street and striking off through side streets, finally stopping at Berner Street. Here, he again stops near a gateway. The entrance to Duffield's Yard. Walks to and fro for a minute or two, then leaves.

2.15 pm – Heads north crossing Commercial Road and enters the Bricklayers Arms in Settle Street. Orders whisky and retires to a quiet corner of the bar. Looks tired, resting his head on his arm. Gets up to leave after ten minutes but is accosted by a man of the costermonger type who calls him by name. Powell rushes out into the street and disappears. Questioned the man, who confirmed that he'd known Powell several years earlier when he frequented the area. Believed him to be a newspaper reporter. 'Years, since I seen him last, owes me five bob, he does. Had two hands in those days.'

Abandoned attempts to find Powell. Proceeded to Whittlesey Street to observe Powell's lodgings.

7.30 pm – No sign of Powell. Observation halted for the day.

"He sets off to Spitalfields and spends hours wandering around Whitechapel. What the hell are we to make of that? Can you make head or tail of it, Alfie?"

"Wondered whether he might be looking for someone, but he didn't knock on the doors of those two houses he stopped at, and the other places were just gateways. Made no sense to me then, and it still doesn't. Knew his way around, though. Along alleyways, through shortcuts, ducking down passages. It was all that I could do to keep him in sight and I know Whitechapel like the back of my hand."

"Then he scurried off when that man called out to him in The Bricklayers Arms. Was it on account of him owing that five bob or was there more to it? Was he worried at being recognised, perhaps?" asked George.

"Really startled him, it did. He high-tailed it out of there. I'm kicking myself for losing him, Mr Benson, but he just seemed to disappear."

"Ah well, no matter. The question is, where did he go? You went straight away to his lodgings?"

"Yes, fast as I could. I'm sure I'd have caught up with him if he'd gone straight back there."

"Well, let's see what today brings. Perhaps Dick will have more luck. What time did he set off this morning?"

"Left home at seven sharp. He'll have been watching the lodgings since half-past."

Chapter 5

George had had a long day. The morning was taken up with inquiries about a missing servant who'd absconded with Lady Graham's pearl necklace and a diamond brooch. Then there was his meeting with Alfie at *The Lamb and Flag*, and the rest of the afternoon was taken up with a debt-collection matter. He'd dined at a chophouse in the Strand, and returned to his office to await Dick, who had instructions to call on him and report on his surveillance of Henry Powell.

"I'll need you to keep an eye on him until midnight, Dick," he'd instructed. "Even if it looks like he's gone home for the evening, just stay and watch in case he comes out again. There's an extra bob or two in it for you. Then come straight here and give me your report."

After writing his notes of the day's activities and preparing some invoices, George settled back in his chair with a decanter of port and *The Illustrated London News*. He'd leafed his way through to page eight, lightly scanning the stories and articles, when his eye was drawn to a lurid sketch purporting to show the discovery of the body of a young woman in Cheapside.

Even though several years had elapsed since the Whitechapel murders, the press still made sensational claims that the Ripper might still be at large. In this case, however, despite the dramatic headline *Ripper Fears as Bloodied Body Discovered*, it transpired that the unfortunate woman's husband had committed the crime in a fit of jealousy and an arrest had been made.

George stared at the page for several minutes before putting the paper to one side and reaching into his desk drawer for the notes he'd discussed with Alfie.

He read carefully through Alfie's account of tailing Henry Powell through the grim streets of the East End. With his fountain pen, he underlined the text in several places, then poured himself another glass of port which he sipped, gazing ruminatively through his window at the streetlamps outside.

He was still in this position five minutes later when the thud of footsteps on the stairs made him turn to face the door. Dick came breathlessly in, red-faced and gabbling.

"Dick, Dick, lad. Sit down and take your time. It's only just turned ten. What's up?"

Dick sat and tried to recover his breath.

"Well, Mr Benson, he's back at the lodgings, but I didn't want to 'ang about on account of what I'd seen at that lock-up of his."

"Now Dick, don't rush, start at the beginning, tell me everything he did. Here you are, have a glass of port."

"Ta, guv. He didn't leave his lodgings till nearly ten this morning. Off he goes towards Waterloo Station, but then he calls in at an ironmonger on Waterloo Road. Quite a big place it is. So I follow him in and pretend to look at some tools."

"Quick thinking, Dick. Did he purchase something?"

"He did. Odd, I thought. What would he want with half a dozen hessian sacks and a length of rope? Anyway, he has it all made up in a bundle, and off he goes."

"Hmm, all right, carry on."

"And then he marches off round the corner of the station and along to a row of lock-ups. It was over an hour before he comes out again."

"What was he doing in there?"

"How should I know? Closed the door behind him, didn't he."

"But Dick, you said you'd hurried here on account of what you'd seen at the lock-up."

"Yeah, that's right, but not then. Later on. It's what I seen later on."

"Right, I understand. But before you tell me that, what else did he do, before you saw him there later?"

"Well, out he comes, as I said, and then I followed him to the Cornwall Arms. It's not far away. Stayed out in the passage, while he goes into the public bar. Then there's all this shouting, so I stick me head round the door and there's a real to-do and no mistake. The barman's coming round the bar and grabbing Powell by the collar. Made myself scarce and waited outside, then out flies Powell with the barman's boot up his jacksie. 'Get out of my pub and don't come back. Try passing forged coins in here again and I'll have the rozzers on ya,' he shouts at him."

"My word, our Mr Powell is a man of many dubious talents, it seems. What next?"

"Picks himself out of the gutter and shouts a few choice words at the barman, but he'd gone back inside. Then off he goes towards the river, crosses Waterloo Bridge and goes into the Embankment Gardens."

"Let me guess, he walked along pretending to be an old soldier and begging from passers-by."

"Yes, he did and all. Pulls this medal out of his pocket and pins it to his lapel. Damned cheek. Worked though, you'd be surprised how many people have got more money than sense."

"So, he made some money, did he?"

"Spent two whole hours at it. Only stopped on account of a bobby happening along. Then he whips the medal off, pockets it and walks away."

"So, it was what, mid-afternoon by this time?"

"About quarter to three, then he heads back over the river and straight to his lodgings. Almost missed him when he came out at five-thirty. All dressed up, he was. Best suit it looked like, tweed overcoat, brown bowler, looked new, and polished boots you could see your face in. Oh, and a flower in his buttonhole."

"A-ha, he was going to meet a woman. At last, we're getting somewhere," George reached for the decanter to refill their glasses. "Carry on Dick, am I right?"

"Well guv, that's what I thought. Off he went back towards the station, but then he turns into *The White Harte* and has his dinner there. Must have done well begging, cos he has several whiskeys to wash it down. Managed to have a bit of food myself, famished I was by then."

"Yes, Dick, I'm sure you were. Was the half-crown I gave you enough for your expenses?"

"Well, it would have been if he'd stopped there but no, off he goes to the Canterbury Theatre so I had to buy a gallery ticket to keep tabs on him and then there's the cab fare to get here as quick as I did. Good job I had some readies of my own."

"Point taken Dick. I'll settle up before you leave. Now, let's see - he goes out all dressed up and has dinner in *The White Harte*, but there's no sign of a woman?"

"No, but you know what some of them Music Halls are like, Mr Benson."

"You mean that ladies of the night were in attendance?"

"Yeah, there's always plenty of tarts around, looking for a bit of business. We wasn't halfway through the programme before he's up out of his seat and watching the ladies parading at the back of the theatre. The Two Aireys was on, trick cyclists. Had to tear myself away and keep an eye on Powell."

"Go on."

"Saw him whispering to a couple of the girls but they didn't seem to take to him. Then, all of a sudden, he's got his arm around this other one and they're off down the stairs."

"Are you telling me he took her to the lock-up?"

"Yeah, he did. Well, that's when it got interesting. They get to the lock-up door, and as he's putting the key in the lock, she takes off. I was standing across the road peering around the corner and she comes running straight at me. Whispers 'e's a wrong un,' as she passes me and keeps running. Damn it all if he doesn't come after 'er."

"Good God, did he catch her?"

"Would 'ave if I 'adn't bumped into 'im. Made out it was all accidental like. Sent him sprawling into the gutter and that's when I saw it."

"What?"

"A knife. Bloody big 'un too. Fell onto the cobbles. Must have had it hidden under his coat. "

"Hell, Dick. Did he try to attack you?"

"No, cursed me to hell and back then picked himself up, which ain't so easy with one hand, and shuffled off. The girl was long gone by then. I followed him from a safe distance 'til he arrived back at his lodgings, then I hailed a cab and came over here."

"Well, there's a lot more to our Mr Powell than I thought. Great work Dick, here's ten bob for now. I'll take over from here. No need for you and Alfie to be involved. Tell Alfie I'll see him at *The Lamb* to settle up."

Chapter 6

Mortimer had just risen from his favourite armchair, intending to go to bed, when the doorbell rang. Muttering a few words of irritation, he shuffled out onto the landing and descended the single flight of stairs to the hallway, his shadow flickering beside him in the gaslight. Who could be calling at this time of night?

"Benson, what the devil brings you here?" he growled testily, then remembered his manners. "Sorry to sound so sharp, old man, just a bit tired. Come on up, will you?"

"Oh well, another small whisky shouldn't hurt. Will you join me?" Mortimer ushered George Benson to an armchair.

George nodded, sinking wearily into the upholstery.

Mortimer handed a glass to him. "Is it the Powell case?"

Mortimer's fatigue was soon forgotten as George apprised him of the events of the past three days. When he'd finished, Mortimer sat back in his chair, digesting the information.

"By God, George, there was I thinking that we had a simple divorce case on our hands, and now what? A thief. A man who passes himself off falsely as a wounded soldier. Forged coins. And that knife. Are we dealing with a dangerous criminal?"

"I fear that we may have one of the most dangerous criminals in London on our hands," George replied.

Mortimer listened as George explained the significance of Powell's mysterious wanderings through Whitechapel two days earlier.

"It was those addresses he visited, Mortimer. I couldn't identify any connection between them when I compiled my notes. Alfie couldn't see any rhyme or reason as to why he stopped at those places either, and it only came to me tonight. Hanbury Street, Millers Court, Buck's Row, Berner Street. They may not ring a bell now, but take yourself back seven years and they were notorious."

"Seven years – 1888? Oh, you mean …"

"The Whitechapel murders. Jack the Ripper. Those were the addresses where the bodies were discovered. Annie Chapman in Hanbury Street, Mary Kelly in Miller's Court, Mary Nicholls in Buck's Row and Elizabeth Stride in Berner Street."

Mortimer replenished their glasses. "There were five, though. Five murders, not four."

"That's right, and I'll wager that it was to that fifth address that Powell went after Alfie lost sight of him. Mitre Square, it's near Aldgate. That's where Catherine Meadows was found."

Mortimer sat bolt upright as the meaning of what he'd just been told sank in.

***

They alighted from a hansom cab outside Waterloo Station at twelve fifty. Three minutes of brisk walking found them standing outside Powell's lock-up, their breath condensing in the night air as they cautiously surveyed their surroundings. Dressed alike in dark overcoats with upturned collars, mufflers, and flat caps pulled well down, they advanced to examine the door lock. The nearest street lamp provided just sufficient light for George to manipulate the lock picks with which he'd become proficient from his time with Pinkerton.

Two minutes later, they were inside, inspecting the interior with the aid of a small lantern that Mortimer had brought. The space measured some thirty feet across, with a curved roof rising to a height of fifteen feet. Holding the lantern aloft, George looked right and left, but was rewarded with no more than dirty brick walls. In front of them, however, stood a wooden partition at least seven feet high, extending from the left-hand wall with a small gap at the other end covered by a stained curtain hanging from an iron rail.

George and Mortimer glanced at one another, then moved cautiously towards the curtain. At a nod from George, Mortimer drew it aside.

A loud shout from the street outside had them spinning around in alarm. It was followed by raucous laughter and a snatch of bawdy singing, which gradually faded away as the revellers went on their way.

Regaining their composure, they returned their attention to the curtained entrance. Mortimer stepped back to let George through, then followed and gazed in astonishment at the scene within.

Against the back wall stood a line of bloody effigies, which, on closer inspection, consisted of scraps of female clothing stretched across wooden frames, like scarecrows - their arms outstretched. Their faces were circles of white card with eyes, noses and mouths crudely painted in black and red. Each countenance was different, but all showed expressions of terror – wide-eyed, with screaming mouths. In daylight, they might almost have looked comical, but in the lantern's glow, they conveyed horror. Their clothes were daubed in slashes of dark red, paint perhaps, or was that blood?

If any doubt remained in the minds of the two onlookers that Powell and the Ripper were one and the same it was soon dispelled. Hanging around the necks of the macabre mannequins were rectangles of cardboard on which were neatly printed the names:
MARY ANNIE ELIZABETH CATHERINE MARY KITTY EVIE

Seven named effigies. And an eighth with no card around its neck.

George found his voice first. "God Almighty, Mallard, it's a chamber of horrors. It's him. Henry Reginald Powell is the Ripper," he whispered hoarsely.

"A simple divorce case, indeed," Mortimer muttered. "Clara, the poor woman, she knows she's married a rogue but never could she have imagined he was this depraved monster."

"Do you see, Mortimer? There are eight. The five he killed back then and three more. And mark the eighth one. It has no name."

"Ah, that woman he brought here. Had she not taken fright, then her name would be facing us, poor soul," Mortimer said gravely.

"Lucky soul, I'd say. And lucky for us too, or perhaps we'd be faced with her dead body as well," George shuddered at the thought.

"I suppose so. Strange though - the Ripper left his victims where he killed them. I mean, he didn't lure them to this place," mused Mortimer.

"Hmm, I wondered about that, too. His modus operandi has changed. Why should that be?"

"And why the hiatus, George? Why did he go to South Africa? Did he turn over a new leaf and if so, why has he returned to his murderous ways?"

As the echo of Mortimer's words died away, their attention shifted to the other features of the chamber. To their left stood a small table with a large paraffin lamp placed upon it and two bentwood chairs. Beyond the table was a narrow iron bedstead covered with a worn grey blanket. A grimy pillow was propped against the bedhead.

"Proper little home from home," George commented sarcastically. "This lamp will give us better light," he added, drawing a box of matches from his coat pocket. In an instant, the room was filled with a steady, bright glow. Bright enough to illuminate a couple of rats scuttling across the floor.

"George, quick, bring that lamp over here." Mortimer's urgency had George striding across the room.

A long, thick wooden bench stood against the side wall. Sturdy, like a woodworker's bench, George thought. Lying on a rectangle of cloth near one end were several knives, a cleaver and two short saws. George reconsidered. No carpenter's tools these. Next to them were two empty enamel bowls and, hanging from an adjacent hook, a butcher's apron. At the other end of the bench, folded neatly, was a pile of hessian sacks upon which rested a coil of rope.

"He was going to cut her up, Mortimer."

Mortimer nodded, pointing shakily at a shelf attached to the wall above the bench. Here, in several glass jars filled with clear liquid, were objects which caused George to stifle a retch. His army life had exposed him to many grim scenes of carnage, but this collection of the Ripper's mementoes had him recoiling in revulsion. Mortimer stood doubled over, vomiting into one of the bowls.

George put the lamp down on the bench, crossed the room and picked up one of the bentwood chairs. "Are you all right, old man?" he said to Mortimer, helping him to sit down, where he remained with his head between his knees, breathing deeply.

George returned to the grim task of inspecting the room. While the items on the bench were arranged neatly, beneath it was a jumble of rubbish, old packing cases, bundles of rags, and paint pots - no doubt those used to decorate the grim effigies.

"Sorry, George, I thought I had a stronger constitution than that." Mortimer got weakly to his feet. "I don't consider myself squeamish, but I suddenly remembered the newspaper reports back then, the missing organs."

"Yes, some of them had parts missing, didn't they?" George replied, glancing back at the shelf. It was then that he noticed it, a flat object lying next to the glass jars, its corner protruding over the edge. Trying to keep his eyes from straying to the jars, George reached up and took hold of it. The book was quarto-sized - a notebook.

Placing it on the bench between the butcher's tools and the oil lamp, he opened the cover.

George thumbed methodically through its contents, with Mortimer looking over his shoulder. Here was further evidence that would deliver Henry Powell to the gallows and damn his soul for all eternity. In neat copperplate, here was the butcher's tally. Each of the murders was described as it had occurred, accompanied by a carefully drawn sketch of the body with a description of the wounds inflicted on it and, most chilling of all, the murderer's comments on how each one had died.

'Sweet as a lamb' or 'Wonderful look of surprise' or 'Bit of a struggler' and so on. George's hand shook as he turned the pages.

The fifth entry gave them a clue as to why the horrors had ceased so abruptly in 1888.

Fought like a tigress. Bitch nearly did for me. Grabbed the knife. Cut my left hand. Nasty wound. Made her pay. Hand's bad, very bad.

Thus ended his description of the murder of Mary Kelly, and he certainly made her pay. Hers was the most gruesome of all the Whitechapel killings.

Mortimer tapped his forefinger on the page. "Could that be it, George? The reason why the murders ceased. She'd cut his left hand, the one that was amputated. It was not lost in a carriage accident as he claimed to Clara. It was because Mary Kelly fought back. Nasty wounds can lead to gangrene can they not?"

"Yes, certainly," George agreed. "Let's suppose, that the loss of his hand caused him to stop. Most of the murders were in public places. He'd have to strike fast, overcome his victim quickly. Not so easy to achieve with a missing hand, and perhaps the shock of someone fighting back also affected him.

"So now he's decided to resume his murdering ways, but with a different approach. He can't risk attacking them in public places anymore, so he lures them here, locks the door so they can't escape and kills them out of sight and sound. Doesn't matter if it's not achieved as quickly, once they're in his power. That would explain the different modus operandi. These new names, Kitty and Evie, murdered and disposed of, and no one the wiser."

"We must go to the police." Mortimer turned away from the grotesque tableau.

"Of course."

Curious to see whether the chamber might have further secrets to reveal, George placed the lamp on the floor while he rummaged in the rubbish piled up under the bench.

"Ahh … the blighter's bitten me!"

As Mortimer spun around, he heard the crash of splintering glass. Then there was a flash as the paraffin spilt from the lamp ignited. George came stumbling towards him, gripping his right wrist.

In an instant, the pile of rubbish caught fire and acrid fumes billowed from the half-full cans of paint.

They retreated to the curtained gap in the partition and watched the flames lick over the bench and across the floor, setting light to the nearest of the mannequins and swiftly engulfing the whole ghastly row.

The fire reached the shelf and threatened to crack the jars.

Mortimer grabbed George by the collar and hurried past the curtain, covering the distance to the lock-up door in rapid strides and stumbling out into the street at the moment that the preservative surrounding the Ripper's grim trophies ignited explosively.

Dazed, they stumbled on until they were a good fifty yards from the lock-up. They watched from a shop doorway as people appeared from all directions, shouting and gesturing.

Some men raced off in search of water, and a bucket chain of sorts was established but, almost as quickly as it had spread, the fire subsided. The solid brick walls of the arched lock-up prevented it from spreading to its neighbours and within minutes, it had consumed all the combustible material within. The air was thick with fumes which had George and Mortimer coughing and covering their mouths and noses with their mufflers.

The distant clanging of a bell, followed by the rattle of hooves and the clatter of wheels over the cobbles, announced the arrival of the fire brigade. As the fire engine drew up, two firemen made for the door while two more started unreeling a hose. Within a few minutes, a fireman emerged from the lock-up waving his hands to signal that the hose would not be needed.

"Come on, Mortimer, let's get a closer look," George urged. They crossed the road to join a small group of bystanders. George wound a handkerchief around his wrist and kept his hand in his pocket.

"All right, the fire's just smouldering a bit now. Smithers, you stay here and keep an eye on it and the rest of you get that hose reeled. We'll be getting back to the station right away," the leading fireman announced. "Not much in there, just a bit of charred furniture and odd bits of scorched wood and rags, some broken glass and bits of metal. The fire was intense while it lasted. There's not much else that I could make out. Good job no one was in there. Hard to say how it could have started, though."

In the hansom cab that carried them back to Mortimer's rooms, the two men sat in dejected silence. They'd found the Ripper, but the evidence of his crimes had gone: the effigies, the awful jars, but most of all the book, the thing that most clearly laid bare Henry Powell's guilt. Now they had nothing to take to the police. The fire would be a setback to his plans, but one day he'd kill again, and perhaps the loss of his lair and its trophies would only serve to spur him on.

Realising that there was little to be gained from dissecting the night's events and both feeling exhausted, they parted, agreeing to meet in Mortimer's office at two that afternoon.

Chapter 7

George hadn't felt such weariness since his army campaigns. Then, it would take days of long dusty route marches, punctuated by short, sharp, adrenaline-charged fighting to induce the bone weariness he now felt.

It wasn't just bodily fatigue that weighed him down, but the knowledge that a golden opportunity to catch the Ripper had slipped away. With slumped shoulders and heedless of his surroundings, he trudged towards his appointment with Mortimer.

That damned rat. The sharp sting of its bite had made George recoil, whipping his hand away by reflex action and sending the lamp flying. If only he'd had the presence of mind to grab that book, the loss of the other evidence wouldn't matter so much. But now there was nothing to connect Henry Powell to the Whitechapel murders. How would the man react, George wondered, when he discovered that his lock-up's contents had been destroyed? Anger, confusion, or maybe even relief?

Mortimer would have every right to be angry with him. He'd certainly be angry if their positions were reversed. What on earth was Mortimer going to tell Clara Powell now?

Enveloped in gloomy speculation, he arrived at Mortimer's chambers and prepared to face the music.

Jimmy led him along the corridor, chirping away about nothing in particular, as was his habit. He opened the door to Mortimer's office with a flourish and ushered George in. The door clicked shut behind him as Jimmy retreated, whistling tunelessly.

Mortimer looked up, setting aside the newspaper he'd been reading. He looked as washed out as George felt. The set of his shoulders, the dark rings around the eyes and the deeply furrowed brow were obvious signs of a troubled mind, but there was more. His eyes reflected deep inner anguish, far more than mere disappointment at the events of the previous night.

"George, please, take a seat. How's your wrist?"

"Oh, I'll live. Cleaned the wound and dressed it myself. That's army training for you," George replied, trying to introduce a note of cheerfulness. "Look, I can't tell you how sorry I am about last night. I'd give the world to set the clock back. If I hadn't been so damned inquisitive, poking about like that, Powell might be in custody by now."

"Come on, man, it was an accident. There's nothing to be gained by a mea culpa. You were right to be inquisitive. It's what I pay you for, after all."

Mortimer hesitated, unsure how to continue, then picked up the folded newspaper lying on the desk in front of him and handed it over. A brief article on page six was circled in ink.

George shook his head as he read the report of the sudden death of a middle-aged woman in Highgate. Mrs Clara Powell had been found dead at home. Her maid had returned from her day off to discover her mistress lying at the foot of the stairs. There were no suspicious circumstances, the article said, and it was presumed that the lady was the victim of an unfortunate accident.

"And there was me wondering what you were going to tell her about our investigation," George said.

"Yes, that had been playing on my mind all night. Well, at least she's been spared the knowledge that her husband's the Ripper. But George, this wasn't an accident, I'm damned sure of it."

"You mean that Powell was behind it? When Alfie lost sight of him, he didn't only call at the site of Catherine Eddowes' murder in Mitre Square, but went on to Highgate?"

Mortimer nodded. "That's it. Your man Alfie was sure he hadn't gone back to his lodgings. Somehow, he gained entry to the house. Who knows, he might have possessed a key. The thing is, George, this has happened before. In South Africa, the rich widow Clara worked for died in the same fashion. I'm convinced that Powell had somehow found out that Clara was to be a beneficiary in that lady's will, even if Clara herself didn't know. It's speculation, of course, and I can't think how we could possibly go about proving any of this. Last night, we discovered that Henry Powell has murdered seven women, but I believe that we can add two more to that tally."

"What now, Mortimer? What the devil are we to do now?"

"Come to dinner tonight, George. There's someone I'd like you to meet."

***

George was surprised to be given an address in Montagu Square as the venue for dinner that evening, rather than

44

Mortimer's Chelsea lodgings. He walked, rather than taking a cab, despite the persistent rain that had been falling since dusk. Shaking his umbrella on the doorstep, he wondered for the umpteenth time why Mortimer had insisted on keeping the identity of the person he was to meet a secret.

He'd thought that it could be a police officer, but this address was too grand for the average inspector. Not the Commissioner, surely? Another lawyer, perhaps, but to what end?

Mortimer himself answered his knock.

"Come in, old man, the weather's turned miserable again." Mortimer helped George with his coat, hat, and umbrella. His mood had lifted since their earlier meeting.

George inspected his surroundings. The hall had a fine Persian carpet running along its length. An oak hallstand stood at one side. Opposite was a mahogany table bearing a Chinese vase and, on the wall above, a gilded circular mirror in the French style. Further along the passage, he glimpsed two framed landscapes of what he imagined were highland scenes. The overall impression was one of refinement and understated wealth, which was reinforced as Mortimer led him into the drawing room.

"George, may I introduce my sister, Verity? Verity, this is my associate, George Benson."

George looked at the young woman standing in the centre of the room. Of medium height, fashionably attired in a light grey silk dress with black embroidery, with her fair hair drawn back in a simple bun. Her most arresting feature was the clarity of her blue eyes, which stared unblinkingly at him. She came forward, extending her hand. "Mr Benson, I've heard so much about you. It's a great pleasure to make your acquaintance."

"The pleasure's all mine, Miss Mallard. However, you do have the advantage over me. Mortimer has never intimated that he had a sister."

"Worried that I might outshine him, no doubt," Verity said breezily, with an amused glance at her brother. "Now, let's not stand on ceremony. Do call me Verity and I will call you George."

George nodded and took a seat. Verity settled herself on a nearby sofa, while Mortimer busied himself with the sherry decanter.

The evening unfolded pleasantly. George gave a potted history of his life. Verity was all curiosity, peppering him with questions and being most intrigued by his time in America. "A Pinkerton man, really? Does that mean you never sleep, George?"

He laughed at her reference to the famous Pinkerton motto.

"I'd hardly call myself a Pinkerton man. I worked for them certainly, but I've never thought of myself as the Pinkerton type. I'm much happier working on my own account."

As he spoke, he was conscious of how little he knew about Mortimer and, of course, his sister, of whom he'd known nothing before this evening.

Verity rose to ring the bell, alerting the kitchen that dinner should be served. "Now George, let's go through to dinner and allow me to tell you a little about us. Clearly, Mortimer has told you very little, if anything. So allow me to enlighten you, and then we will discuss the little matter of a business proposition."

"George," Verity began as the soup was served, "Mortimer and I are not merely siblings but twins. I, quite properly, was born first, with Mortimer trailing some way behind, as has been his habit ever since."

George chuckled, glancing across at Mortimer, who rolled his eyes.

"I earn my living as a journalist. You may have seen my column on London life from a woman's perspective in *The London Journal*. No? Well, promise me you'll look it up. It's very popular, you know. Then there's *The Englishwoman's Review*, of course. You may as well know I'm a keen supporter of women's suffrage. I realise that may sound terribly worthy, but the justice of our cause is indisputable and the day when we women are afforded the fundamental right to vote may be closer than you think."

"I dare say you're right Verity," George replied. He privately thought that denying half the population the vote was wrong. On the other hand, it wasn't a subject that he felt in any way passionate about, indeed, he seldom thought about it at all.

"Of course, I'm right, George and bravo, by the way, for managing to avoid the usual male expressions of condescension about my being a journalist."

"Verity also has the distinction of having obtained a Bachelor of Arts degree from the University of London," Mortimer interjected. "Her talents are quite unbounded," he added with a wink.

"Very well, Mortimer, I'll stop talking about myself. Perhaps you would like to add something," Verity retorted.

"Well, George already knows the essentials where I'm concerned."

"Yes, I suppose so, but have you both always lived in London? This house is a very fine establishment," George said.

"We are country folk at heart, aren't we, Verity? Our family home is near Flaxminton in Oxfordshire. Our father is the rector there. This is our, or should I say, his, townhouse."

George looked around the dining room, noting the quality of the furniture and furnishings.

"George is wondering how a country rector can possibly be the owner of this place. Isn't that right George?" said Verity, regaining control of the conversation as she invariably did. "You see, our father is the Reverend Sir Stanmore Mallard, sixth Baronet. As a second son, he went into the Church, but succeeded to the baronetcy when his brother succumbed to an unfortunate disease of what we might politely call a social nature."

"Thank you, sister, for your customary candour," Mortimer said, shaking his head. "Perhaps it's time to take the conversation in another direction."

The next hour passed swiftly with Verity very much in control of the discussion: music, the new Tower Bridge, social conditions in the East End, and the latest gossip about the Prince of Wales. She led them effortlessly from topic to topic until dinner was over and they retired to the more intimate ambience of the drawing room. Whisky and soda being the order of the day, they settled back in their chairs.

"Verity, you may as well have the floor, as it's your proposal," Mortimer opened.

"Very well. Now, George, do you believe in justice?"

George blinked, wondering where on earth this was leading.

"Of course, doesn't everyone?" he responded warily.

"But what is justice, George? It's not a trick question; really, what is it?"

"Well, I suppose it means that criminal acts should be punished."

"Yes, I see. You equate justice with punishment. Hmm, in the sixteenth century, it was considered just to burn religious dissenters at the stake, and it's only a little over sixty years ago that burglary was routinely punished by hanging."

"Let's say, then, that the punishment should fit the crime. After all, times have changed."

"Yes, they have, but there remain crimes, or at least one crime, which would still be very properly regarded as meriting the death sentence. The punishment for murder does indeed fit the crime, does it not, George? Furthermore, if a murderer is not punished in that way, wouldn't that, in itself, be unjust?"

"Go on."

"Consider a man who is known to have committed not one but seven heinous murders."

"Nine actually," Mortimer chipped in. 'He did for Clara and that old lady in South Africa, too.'

"Yes, I take your point, brother, but is it not the case that you and George have only seen evidence that Henry Powell committed seven murders, the original Whitechapel murders and two more recent ones?"

"Very, well, seven proven heinous murders it is," Mortimer conceded

"Ah yes, and there lies the problem. You say they are proven, but the proof no longer exists. As a lawyer, you know full well that there's no evidence upon which to justify a charge of murder and no chance at all of a conviction. If you and George were to go to the police stating that you had seen such evidence, despite the fact that you are of impeccable character, it would simply be regarded as hearsay, would it not? And then there is the rather tricky issue of how you came to be inside the lock-up and how its contents came to catch fire. To the police, it would appear that the only crimes committed were by you and George, to-wit, breaking and entering, and arson."

"Indeed. You sum up the position perfectly, Verity. We find ourselves in a quandary. We know that Henry Powell is the Ripper and we also know that he'll kill again. If we do nothing, a new terror will be unleashed. Which is why, George, Verity and I have decided that if justice cannot be served through the usual channels, then unorthodox methods are called for."

As the discussion went back and forth between Verity and Mortimer, George felt the muscles in his neck tightening as the nature of their 'business proposition' dawned on him. Not only were they indicating their intent to kill Henry Powell, but they also wanted him to be an accomplice. He'd done some dirty work in his time at Pinkerton and he'd committed many acts in his army career that would not be tolerated in civilian life. But to kill calculatedly and deliberately?

Verity and Mortimer waited for his reaction.

"So, you're proposing to become the instruments of justice: police, judge, jury and executioner, all in one. And you want me to be part of it. What makes you think that I won't go to the police and tell them that I've discovered a conspiracy to commit murder?"

"Would you George? If you're truly the man that Mortimer tells me you are, is that at all likely?" Verity said.

"We wouldn't have dreamed of involving you if we thought that you'd go running to the police. Your sense of justice is as strong as ours, isn't it?"

George smiled. "It'll take more than flattery or some wide-eyed appeal to my finer instincts to get me involved in your little plan, Verity. Yes, I grant you that I'm as keen as you to make sure that this creature doesn't kill again, but let's not pretend that there's not another motive here."

"Go on," Verity returned George's smile.

"With due respect to your undoubted talents, Verity, I don't believe that physically restraining and dispatching a strong and dangerous man is one of them. Mortimer is handy enough in his way, but the thought of the two of you attempting such a thing is quite preposterous. Which is why you need me. Mind you, after my encounter with that rat last night, I wouldn't blame you for having second thoughts."

"Yes, George," Mortimer conceded, "you're right, of course, although you might be surprised at what Verity and I are capable of. Nevertheless, we need someone with the knowledge and experience to bring this off in such a way that we're never suspected."

"The stakes couldn't be higher, Mortimer. If we fail, it will be our necks in a noose."

Chapter 8

Henry Powell's world had been turned upside down. His plan to continue his murderous career had collapsed. It all depended on the lock-up. It was both a shrine and the place where he could safely dispatch his victims.

The loss of his hand all those years ago gravely damaged his confidence and had, for a time, even quenched the urge to kill. He'd genuinely felt a sense of release in South Africa. New beginnings in a sunny climate, with blue skies instead of the fog-shrouded grime of London, had brought a sense of hope. He'd felt genuine affection for Clara. The circumstances in which she had become quite wealthy, circumstances which he'd helped to bring about by pitching that old woman downstairs, offered a golden opportunity to leave his past behind for good.

Except that his lost hand was a daily reminder of his past. A need for revenge brooded in his subconscious.

If only they'd stayed in Cape Town.

London and all its old associations reclaimed him. It took some time but, bit by bit, the old Henry returned. When Clara threw him out, his regression was complete.

He'd rented the lock-up in a false name and paid the rent scrupulously by postal order. There was nothing to link him to it.

When he took his usual route past Waterloo Station the following afternoon, it had come as an enormous shock to find the place crudely cordoned off with lengths of timber nailed across the damaged front entrance. The remains of the door, which stood ajar, showed signs of severe charring, with the green paint blistered and cracked.

Immediately wary, he kept walking, casting a glance into the acrid-smelling interior as he passed. The wooden partition was largely destroyed. The secrets it once concealed were reduced to a blackened, melted mess.

Crossing the road, he stopped at the nearest street corner, pretending to examine the window display at the haberdasher's there. His mind raced as he calculated the chances that anything in the lock-up could be associated with him. The fire had been intense enough to obliterate the effigies and the jars with their hideous contents. The notebook was his chief concern. Surely it would have been destroyed? Of course, it must have been.

But how did the fire start? It could hardly ignite spontaneously. Had someone broken in? He looked across to the partly open door. The worst of the damage, the badly charred area where the timbers had completely burned away, was on the right side - where the lock had been. He'd no way of knowing whether it had been picked or broken.

The woman, that damned tart he'd picked up in the *Canterbury*, could she have something to do with it? She'd turned tail and fled just as he'd put his key in the lock. He thought of going to the Canterbury again that night to silence her, but quickly put it aside. After all, she didn't know his name or where he lived. Maisie was the name she gave him, the name that would have appeared around the neck of that eighth effigy.

With his mind still ranging over the possibility of anything incriminating him, he entered a nearby newsagent and tobacconist shop. Requesting a packet of pipe tobacco, he made a casual enquiry.

"Looks like there's been a fire over there," he said, holding out his good hand for his change.

"Had us out of bed, it did. A right to-do, and no mistake. Me and my lad Eddie ran over to see what we could do, but it was all over bar the shouting by then. Fire brigade was too late, as usual."

"Anyone know who owns it?" Henry asked.

"Nah, no idea. Could be anyone. Why d'you ask?"

"Oh, no reason."

"Well, there was nothing much in there, I can tell you that. Eddie went back over first thing this morning and had a good nose around. Just a few sticks of burnt furniture, he said. Bits of charred timbers, broken glass, that sort of thing. Some knives too, but the handles were all burnt, so he left them there. It's all boarded up now."

He knew as he walked away that there was nothing for it. He'd have to move again. Back north of the river. Not Paddington, some other borough where he'd not be recognised. Meanwhile, he'd stay far away from Waterloo Station.

A week passed and Henry progressed gradually from a state of panic to a sense that all might be well after all. The fire had attracted no interest from the newspapers. In the scheme of things, it was unremarkable, lost in the torrent of daily events across the metropolis. He had two major concerns. The first was to find a regular source of income. The second was to satisfy his urge to kill.

Chapter 9

Henry spent an entire week in Fleet Street and roundabout, trying to find work. He avoided any newspapers where he thought the editors might know of his dubious reputation. There were more of them than he realised and on the rare occasions where he was granted an audience with the editor, he found himself rebuffed.

After another fruitless morning, he retired to *The Old Bell* to lick his wounds and dull his disappointment with alcohol. He occupied a quiet corner of the bar, alone with his thoughts, and felt irritated to see two men seating themselves at the next table.

At first, he considered finishing his drink and moving on, but the drumming of the rain on the window behind him changed his mind.

He turned his attention to the two interlopers. The younger man, in a frock coat, looked to be in his late twenties. His top hat rested on an empty chair at his side, against which was propped a silver-topped cane. His companion, in a tweed suit and bowler hat, he estimated at thirty-five. Journalistic curiosity overcame his resentment as he sat eavesdropping. He'd not seen either before. They weren't among the regulars, who were mainly hacks or city clerks.

"I'm seeing his lordship this evening, Angus. He's getting rather fractious. We're still a couple of reporters short. You'll have to plug the gaps by the end of the week or he'll lose patience," the younger man said in a patrician drawl.

"Look, Geoffrey, if we were seeking common or garden hacks, there'd be no problem. You know as well as I do that the types we're after aren't that easy to come by, not if they're any good, anyhow," Angus responded in an American accent.

"You mean not if they're any bad, don't you?" Geoffrey sniggered.

"There's Chegwin at the *Exposé*. He'd sell his grandmother for sixpence, but he told me where to go in no uncertain terms when I broached the subject."

"Discreetly, I hope."

"Of course, discreetly. Don't worry, his lordship's plans haven't been compromised. Thought you knew me better than that," Angus snapped.

"All right, all right. Point taken. Here, get us a drink, would you?" Geoffrey placed a coin on the table.

Angus shrugged, picked up the coin, and made his way to the bar. Watching his broad back as he pushed his way past a couple of patrons, Geoffrey leaned back, folding his arms, his brow furrowed in thought.

A low cough to his right made him sit up.

"Oh, didn't see you sitting there. I do hope my colleague and I didn't disturb you," he said pleasantly. "Just some tedious business matters, nothing of any importance," he added, turning his head away.

"Yes, I couldn't help hearing," Henry said. "Don't get me wrong, sir, it's none of my business, of course, but am

I right in thinking that your colleague is in the newspaper trade?"

Geoffrey turned back to face him. "You're quite right, my good man. It is none of your business," he said sharply.

"Shame, just thought I could help, being in that line of business myself. Not much I don't know about Fleet Street."

"So you say. However, you seem to have the wrong end of the stick. We do not require your assistance, I can assure you. Ah, there you are, Angus," he called out, seeing his companion approaching with full glasses. "Let's move somewhere more private."

Angus put the glasses down. "What's the problem, Geoffrey? The place is quite full, you know, I doubt we'll find another table. Is it this fellow?" he said, nodding in Henry's direction.

"Begging your pardon. I was just telling this gentleman that I'm very well acquainted with Fleet Street, being a journalist myself, if you're looking for someone, I ..."

Geoffrey snapped, "Damn it, man, I just told you ..."

"Whoa, hold your horses there. I'm the one who makes the decisions when it comes to hiring." Angus resumed his seat and turned to face Henry. "You were saying?"

"Oh, well, I was saying that if you're looking for a reliable man who knows the ropes, I'm considering new opportunities myself. The name's Powell, Henry Powell."

"I see, Mr Powell. Not working at the moment, are you?"

"Been doing some freelance work, needed some time to devote to other business, so I couldn't take on a full-time job. But that's all done with now. It's fortuitous that you've caught me at the right time before I take up other offers."

"Really Mr Powell, you appear to take a great deal for granted, as you know nothing about us or any interest we may or may not have in employing any journalist. However, I'll concede that we are in the market for the right sort of person. I'll tell you what, we'll consider what you've just told us and if we're interested in speaking with you again, we'll contact you. If you would kindly provide me with your address, I'll be in touch. Expect a telegram tomorrow. Now, if you'd be so good as to give my colleague and me some privacy, we'd be much obliged."

Henry took a scrap of paper from his pocket and retrieved a pencil stub to scrawl down his address; handing it to Angus, he shuffled through the bar and out into the street.

Mortimer and George watched him go, then clinked their glasses together in a silent toast.

Chapter 10

The telegram the next day was brief.

PROSPECT OF WHITBY 9 PM

That was all. Henry knew the pub. He'd been there once or twice. On Wapping Wall, right by the Thames. Strange place to meet, he thought, but if discretion was the aim, away from the prying eyes of Fleet Street, then it was as good as anywhere.

He almost lost his way in the fog and had to ask a passer-by for directions, fearing that he'd be late for his appointment. He'd spent the day musing about what sort of opportunity might be in the offing. Both Geoffrey and Angus were strangers to him, and he'd been most intrigued by the mention of 'his lordship.' The world of Grubb Street was full of newspapers and periodicals that came and went. If Lord someone or other with more money than sense was keen to add another, good luck to him. The main thing was that if the men involved in this venture were new on the scene, then, although he knew nothing of them, they hopefully knew little, if anything, about him.

He inhaled a thick mixture of smoke, ale, old timber and pitch as he crossed the threshold. The pub was well patronised but not full. Popular with river workers: lightermen, stevedores and the like. He consulted his watch and scanned the bar, but saw no sign of Geoffrey or Angus. Two minutes past nine. Perhaps they'd been delayed.

A hand gripped his shoulder.

Little wonder he'd not seen them. Angus stood next to him wearing a reefer jacket with the collar turned up and a peaked black cap, looking every inch the riverboat skipper. He gestured towards a table in a corner of the room where Geoffrey sat, similarly dressed, with a blue woollen cap pulled down over his head.

A bottle of rum occupied the centre of the table with three full glasses.

Geoffrey broke the silence. "Capital. I see our little effort at disguise had the desired effect. We're most keen to keep our business a secret for the present, hence our choice of venue and dress. Now, Mr Powell, you'll be so good as to keep silent while Angus here describes the type of journalist we're looking for. It will then be up to you to convince us whether you are that person."

"Mr Powell, Henry, you're a man of experience, or so you tell us. That being the case, you'll appreciate that the public has an unquenchable taste for the more sensational aspects of human life. Scandal, criminality, gossip, rumour, innuendo, anything which excites, titillates, horrifies, and blunts the tedious reality of everyday life. The more fantastic the better, and if it involves the famous and the upper classes, then bingo, we have a little goldmine on our hands," Angus whispered, leaning across the table.

"There's many a scandal rag already," Henry responded.

"Indeed, there are, Henry. It's a crowded field, I grant you. Now I'm not from hereabouts, it's obvious from my accent. I'm American. Spent my whole career along the east coast. New York, Philadelphia, Boston, you name it. So,

I'm not interested in how things are done here in good old London town. I'm here to shake things up, Henry. Our little venture will get down deeper in the gutter than anyone's done before. We'll be more cunning, more ruthless, more imaginative than the rest. We'll get the stories that matter and we'll get them first and if we have to make 'em up, we'll do that better than anyone else. We'll be the paper everyone's talking about. If you've got the right stuff, Henry, you can be part of it."

Henry listened as Angus went on enthusiastically extolling the commercial soundness of the venture and his own unparalleled talents as the editor designate. His American brashness and self-confidence chipped away at Henry's hard-bitten scepticism until he found himself imagining a bright future as a star reporter. He'd nothing to lose, anyway.

Now it was Henry's turn. He'd rehearsed a story in which he'd worked long and hard in Fleet Street, outshining many of his contemporaries and attracting their enmity. Without making it too much of a hard-luck tale, he intimated that professional jealousy had unfairly undermined him and it was that which prompted his move to South Africa, where his talents had met with the recognition they deserved. Here he felt on firm ground, embellishing his tale in the hope that his claims would not be tested.

Angus listened. His face, devoid of expression, gave no clue as to his thoughts.

"So, why'd you come back, Henry, since you were doing so well?" he asked suddenly.

Henry was ready for that. He talked about how he'd met, courted, and married a woman in Cape Town and had returned at her behest, but in this version of the tale, it was on account of her having developed consumption and her desire to die in England. He gave it just the right amount of emotion, he thought, without descending into self-pity. The message was that he'd sacrificed a glowing future for love. And in this version, his wife was called Edna.

Geoffrey and Angus made the usual expressions of sympathy. Then Angus looked him in the eye, "Okay Henry, that's all well and good, but we're looking for a hard-nosed, stop at nothing, downright bastard, is that you?"

That was all he needed to play his trump card; no pretence necessary. For the next twenty minutes, he trawled through his past, all the times he'd duped and exploited people, traded in their misery, made promises he'd no intention of keeping, ruined reputations and twisted the truth. He painted the picture they wanted to see. He was a thoroughly unscrupulous man - but they'd never know just how bad he really was.

They heard him out in silence.

He finished and looked at Angus, but it was Geoffrey who spoke, "Be a good chap and take a turn outside, would you, Mr Powell? Have a smoke while we confer."

Henry shuffled out into the street. The fog had closed in, a thick grey-black mixture of river mist and smoke; it clung to him. Buttoning his overcoat against the chilly night air, he reached into his pocket and withdrew his pipe, then performed the awkward process of one-handedly filling and lighting it. He'd no idea how long their conferring would take, but as he stood puffing on his sweet tobacco mixture, he allowed himself to hope that something would come of it. A job, an income, and if what they said was true about the tawdry nature of their publication, then he was the right man for it.

What was taking so long? The cold seeped into his boots. He stamped up and down, walking a few paces one way, then the other. A couple of times he'd thought his ordeal had ended when the pub door opened, but it was only other patrons leaving.

At last, Angus beckoned in the doorway. Henry glanced at his pocket watch – twelve minutes past ten.

Seated again at the table, he waited for the verdict. By now, he was cold and irritated. If the answer was no, he'd not take it calmly. They'd get the full blast of his temper, even if it caused a scene. He'd not be trifled with by these two or his so-called lordship.

Angus held out his hand. "Okay, Henry, you're our man. Shake on it."

Henry's annoyance evaporated. He took the proffered hand and shook it warmly. He looked over at Geoffrey, expecting a similar gesture, but received only a curt nod.

"Now then, a toast," Angus continued, "to a profitable association. Let's show Fleet Street how it's done."

The glasses of rum had remained untouched since Henry's original arrival. He'd looked longingly at the dark liquid several times during his interview, but as neither Geoffrey nor Angus showed any inclination to take a sip, he followed their lead. Now all three lifted their glasses and drained them.

Angus refilled their glasses. "Tell me, Henry, the hand, how'd you lose it?"

The American's directness took Henry aback for an instant. "Oh, that happened in South Africa. My wife and I were set upon by a group of drunken Boer farmers. We were out driving when they accosted us. She was terrified. I took my whip to the ringleader and then they were on me. Put two of them on their backs, but one of them took a swing at me with an axe. They ran off then, and I owe my life to Edna, who had the presence of mind to drive us back to Cape Town post haste. My life was saved but my hand couldn't be." He had several versions of how his hand was lost, which he used as best suited the occasion. This one, he felt, was just right for Geoffrey and Angus.

Angus emitted a low whistle, and Geoffrey nodded condescendingly. They seemed to regard him with more respect. The formal business of the evening over, they fell to small-talk and tittle-tattle. Even Geoffrey's icy reserve melted a little.

The bottle was almost drained. Henry had a good head for liquor, but tonight he felt light-headed. It couldn't be the rum. Perhaps that spell outside and the sudden return to the warmth of the bar accounted for it. He was tired now and somewhat daunted by the prospect of getting back to Southwark.

"I think I'll be off," he mumbled drowsily.

"Of course, Henry, and we'll be glad to get you a cab and see you home, but there's just one more little thing before we can consider our deal to be done."

"What thing? I thought we were finished here. You saying I haven't got the job?" Henry growled.

"Not at all, but there's someone that needs to give his blessing, a mere formality of course, and he's the one who will advance you a bonus for signing up for our venture."

"Bonus, how much? Who's this someone? Is he here? Where is he?"

Henry was in difficulty. He was confused, slurring his words. His head ached.

"A very attractive bonus," Angus replied. "You needn't worry about that, but it's in the gift of his lordship. Now, we're just going to cross the river. His lordship has a discrete residence in Rotherhithe. Keeps one of his mistresses there. We've got a boat, just a few minutes straight across, and then we can complete the business. Geoffrey here rowed at Oxford. He'll have us there in no time."

"Just a few minutes? River?" Henry muttered. His vision was blurred. Angus and Geoffrey helped him to his feet and walked him slowly to the door. "Come along, old chap, it's not far," Angus said soothingly. Their exit passed unnoticed. It was late, and the sight of an inebriated patron being helped to leave was nothing unusual.

The fog enveloped them as they made their way down to the riverbank to a landing stage where a small wooden rowing boat lay tied up, bobbing gently. Henry was barely aware of his surroundings. His limbs felt heavy. It was all he could do to put one foot in front of the other. But for the firm grip that Angus and Geoffrey had on his arms, he'd have sunk to the ground.

A perilous couple of minutes passed as he was manoeuvred carefully into the boat with his companions struggling to support his weight and keep their balance. At last, they had him seated in the stern. Angus sat next to him, keeping him upright with an arm around his shoulders, while Geoffrey untied the painter and pushed off with an oar.

Practically insensible, his head lolled on Angus's shoulder. His bowler hat fell off and bounced off the thwart into the Thames, disappearing instantly into the gloom. The chloral hydrate, with which Angus had laced his first glass of rum, had done its work. His breathing was slow and laboured under the effect of the powerful sedative, his limbs slack.

The boat reached the middle of the Thames tideway. Geoffrey stopped rowing and pulled the oars inboard. As it bobbed in the stream, he moved gingerly to the stern. While Angus maintained a firm grip on Henry, Geoffrey reached into his jacket and withdrew a small, stoppered bottle and a thick cotton wad.

Kneeling carefully, he withdrew the stopper and soaked the wad with its contents.

One second was all the warning they had of the vessel's approach. A shadow loomed above them and only then did they hear the dull throb of its engine. Geoffrey toppled backwards, dropping the chloroform bottle and watching helplessly as the vessel scraped across their bow, sending them spinning away but undamaged, save for some scratches. Had its course been a mere foot to port, they would have been upended. As suddenly as it had appeared, the vessel was past them, its crew unaware of their presence.

"Are you alright?" Angus whispered urgently to Geoffrey, digging his fingers into Henry's arms to keep him upright.

Geoffrey struggled to resume his place. The wad was still in his hand. He reached down to retrieve the bottle which had spilt some of its contents. "Damn," he whispered, hoping that there would be enough to do the job.

He leaned forward, pressing the cotton wad firmly over Henry's mouth and nose. To his relief, there was no reaction. Henry remained motionless in Angus's grip. In normal circumstances, chloroform could take several minutes to act, but since Henry was already sedated, he soon lapsed fully into unconsciousness. Alert to the possibility of another vessel approaching, Angus and Geoffrey strained their ears for any sound. There was nothing.

Geoffrey lifted Henry's legs, gradually tipping his limp body backwards over the stern, guided by Angus, making sure that his descent into the Thames produced no splash. The body sank briefly beneath the water, then surfaced facedown alongside the boat. Geoffrey applied the blade of an oar to Henry's back and pressed down, watching until the last bubbles of air had gone.

Within three strokes of the oars, they lost sight of Henry Powell's mortal remains.

Their alter egos drifted away with Henry's body. They became Mortimer and George once more.

"A more merciful end than he showed his victims," George said as they approached the bank, with no trace of the American accent he'd convincingly employed as Angus.

"May he never rest in peace," was Mortimer's only comment.

***

Dan Hobson peered through the dawn mist. He held the wheel firmly as he guided his tug and its string of empty barges downriver. A veteran of the Thames, he knew better than to let his eyes wander and kept a narrow focus on the water dead ahead. Had he ventured a glance to starboard, he might have glimpsed an object bobbing on the surface. As it was, he remained unaware of the body as it bumped along the side of his vessel, encased in a thick tweed overcoat that snagged on a splinter of timber near the stern. The accidental passenger rode down the Thames as far as Gravesend. There, the wash from a passing vessel detached it from Dan's tug, giving it up to the tide which took it out into the chill emptiness of the North Sea. It sank without trace.

Acknowledgements

With thanks to Ian Hooper and all at Book Reality for making this book a reality.

About The Author

R J Williams was born in Aberystwyth in Wales and now lives in Perth, Western Australia.

After a busy career in information technology and management consulting, in the UK and Australia, retirement has given him the opportunity to indulge his interest in history and pursue his long-held ambition to become an author of historical novels.

He enjoys writing, cycling, travelling, and volunteering with Para Quad industries, who provide employment to people with disabilities.